GRAPHIC MYTHICAL CREATURES

SEA MONSTERS

BY GARY JEFFREY

ILLUSTRATED BY TERRY RILEY

Gareth Stevens
Publishing

Please visit our website, www.garethstevens.com.
For a free color catalog of all our high-quality books,
call toll free 1-800-542-2595 or fax 1-877-542-2596.

Library of Congress Cataloging-in-Publication Data

Jeffrey, Gary.
Sea monsters / Gary Jeffrey.
p. cm. — (Graphic mythical creatures)
Includes index.
ISBN 978-1-4339-6043-7 (pbk.)
ISBN 978-1-4339-6044-4 (6-pack)
ISBN 978-1-4339-6041-3 (library binding)
1. Sea monsters. I. Title.
GR910.J45 2011
398.24'54—dc22

2010052608

First Edition

Published in 2012 by
Gareth Stevens Publishing
111 East 14th Street, Suite 349
New York, NY 10003

Copyright © 2012 David West Books

Designed by David West Books
Editor: Ronne Randall

Printed in China

CPSIA compliance information: Batch #DS11GS: For further information contact Gareth Stevens, New York, New York at 1-800-542-2595.

CONTENTS

SERPENTS AND SEA BEASTS
4

HERCULES AND THE SEA MONSTER
6

MORE SEA MONSTER STORIES
22

GLOSSARY
23

INDEX
24

Serpents and Sea Beasts

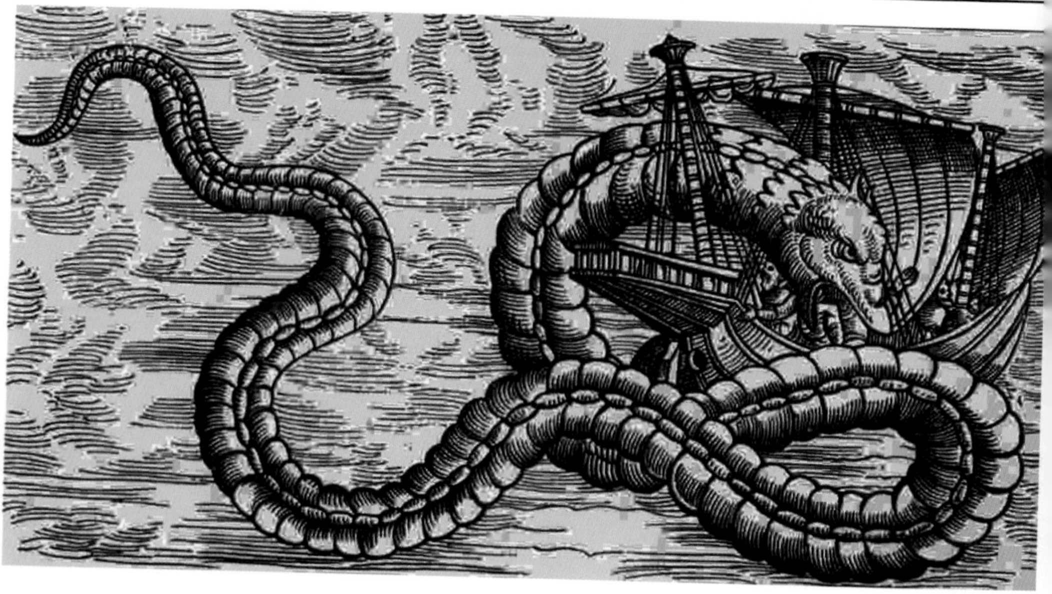

The deep mystery and danger of the world's oceans have worried the imaginations of seafarers since ancient times. Sea monster stories feature the largest and most terrifying of all mythical creatures.

This 16th-century woodcut imagines a coiled sea serpent who is mad and hungry for people.

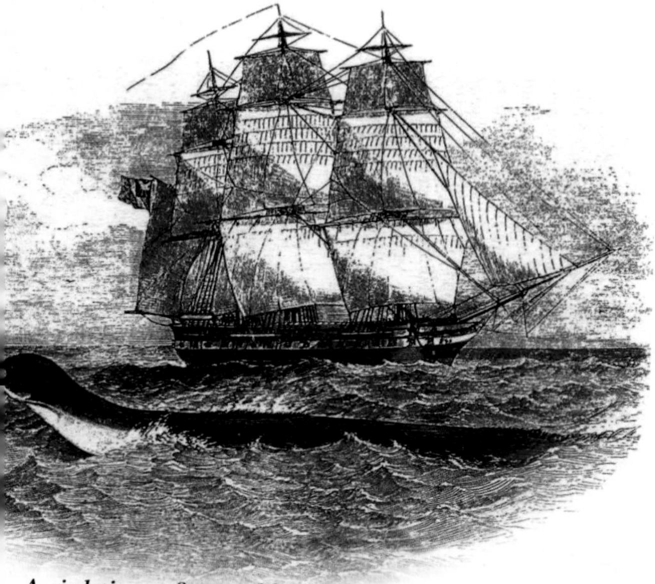

A sighting of a real-life sea serpent was reported by the crew of HMS Daedalus in 1848.

Leviathan

Leviathan was an ancient sea monster who caused chaos. Monsters like Leviathan are often linked to whales. Other monsters are linked to sea serpents—huge, scaly creatures who rise up out of the ocean to spout water at passing ships, or worse.

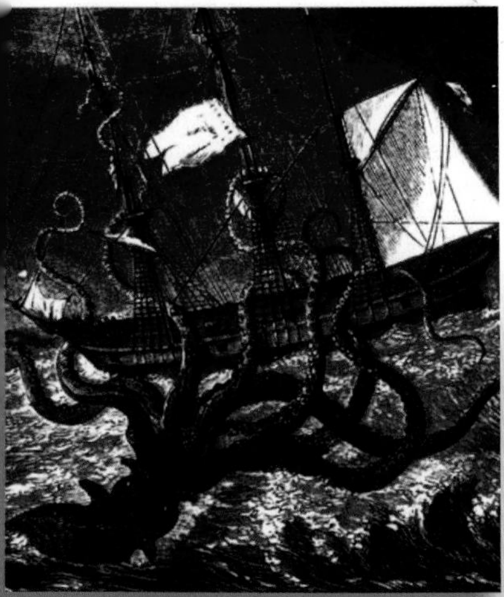

Sightings of real-life giant squid in the 19th century inspired images like this.

Kraken

So large that it was sometimes mistaken for an island, the Kraken is a scary octopus-like creature that attacks ships. Stories about Kraken came from Scandinavia, where whirlpools and odd currents were explained away as the underwater movements of these huge, writhing beasts.

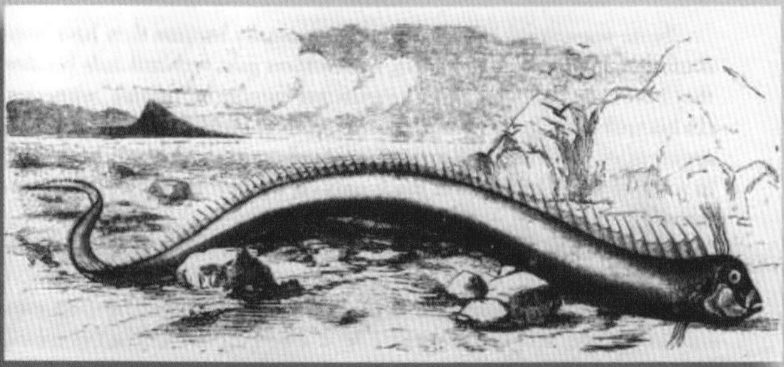

Strange real-life creatures like the giant oarfish have been mistaken for sea monsters.

Lake Monsters

Sightings of lake monsters have been reported across North America and Europe for centuries. Some people think they may be prehistoric survivors, others that they are misidentified… or hoaxes.

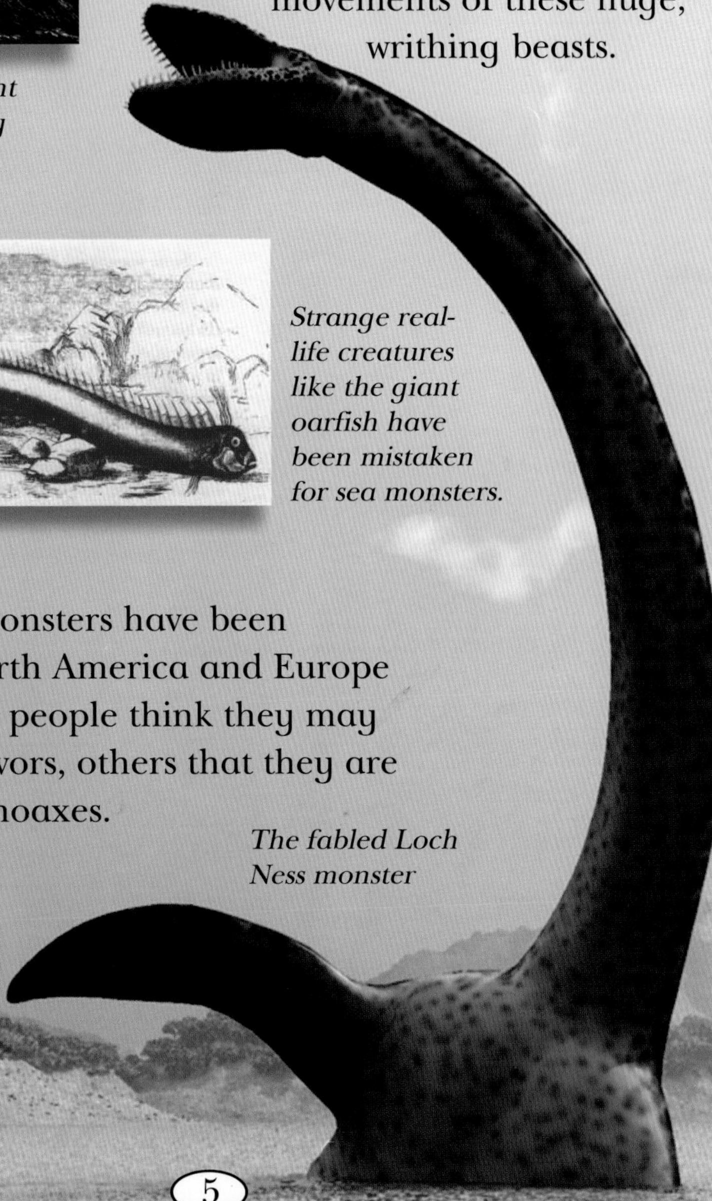

The fabled Loch Ness monster

HERCULES AND THE SEA MONSTER

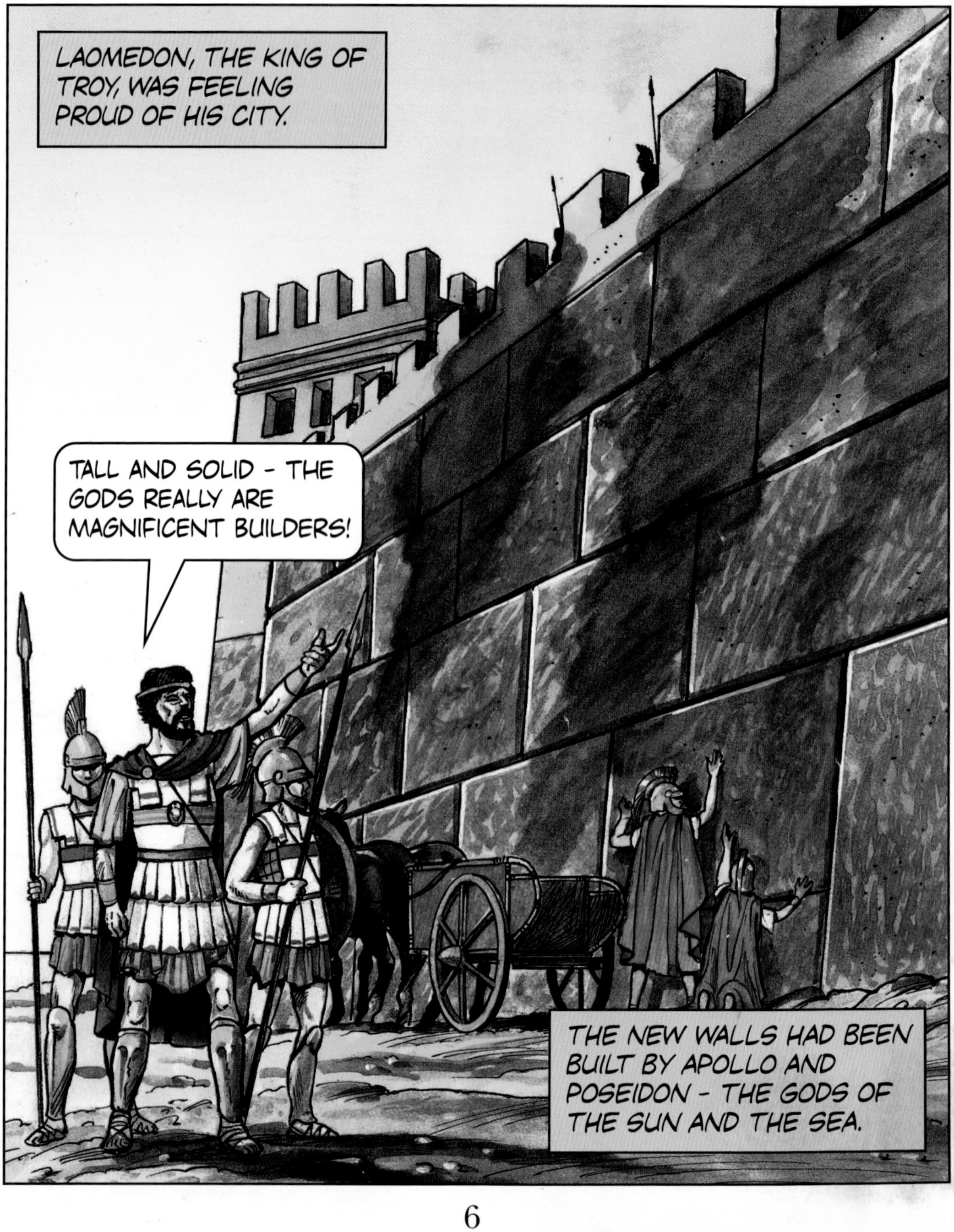
LAOMEDON, THE KING OF TROY, WAS FEELING PROUD OF HIS CITY.
TALL AND SOLID - THE GODS REALLY ARE MAGNIFICENT BUILDERS!
THE NEW WALLS HAD BEEN BUILT BY APOLLO AND POSEIDON - THE GODS OF THE SUN AND THE SEA.

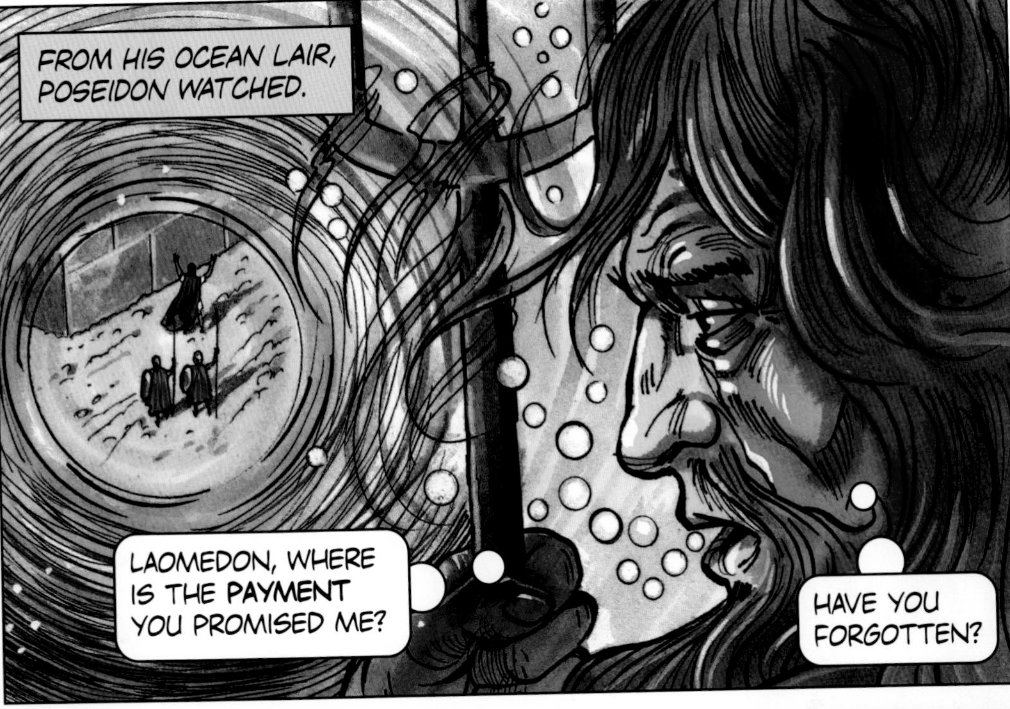
FROM HIS OCEAN LAIR, POSEIDON WATCHED.
LAOMEDON, WHERE IS THE **PAYMENT** YOU PROMISED ME?
HAVE YOU FORGOTTEN?

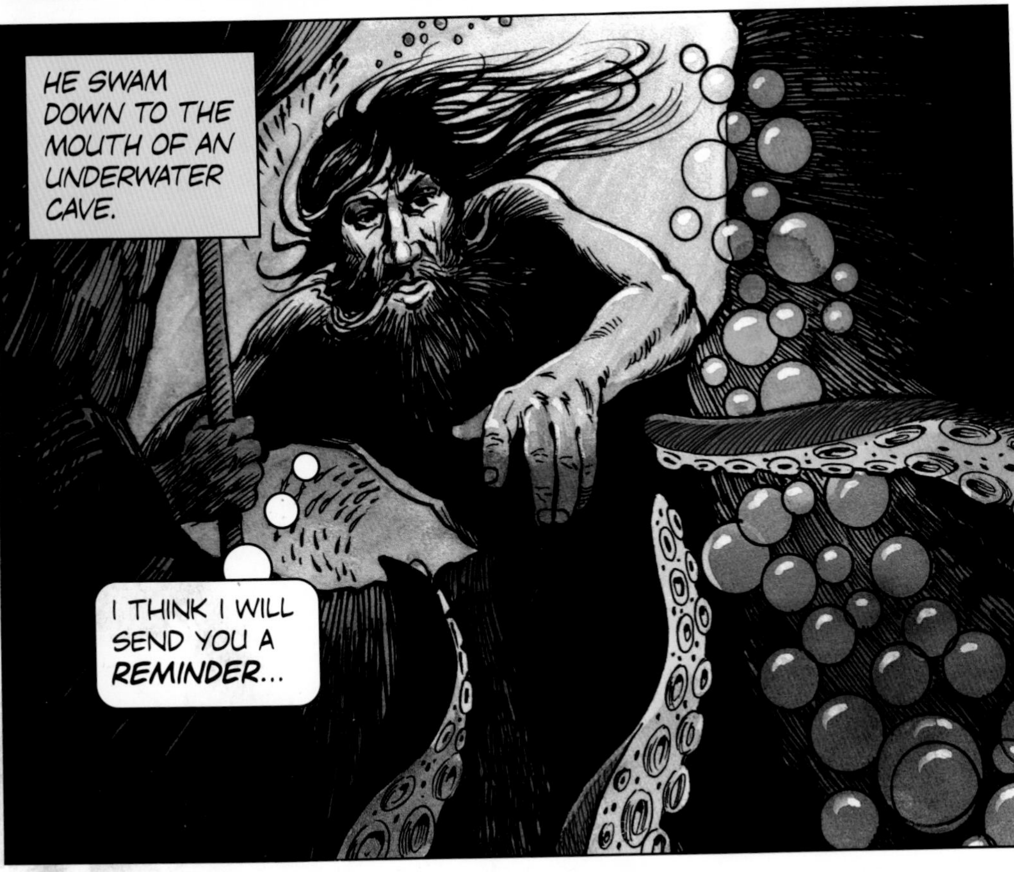
HE SWAM DOWN TO THE MOUTH OF AN UNDERWATER CAVE.
I THINK I WILL SEND YOU A ***REMINDER***...

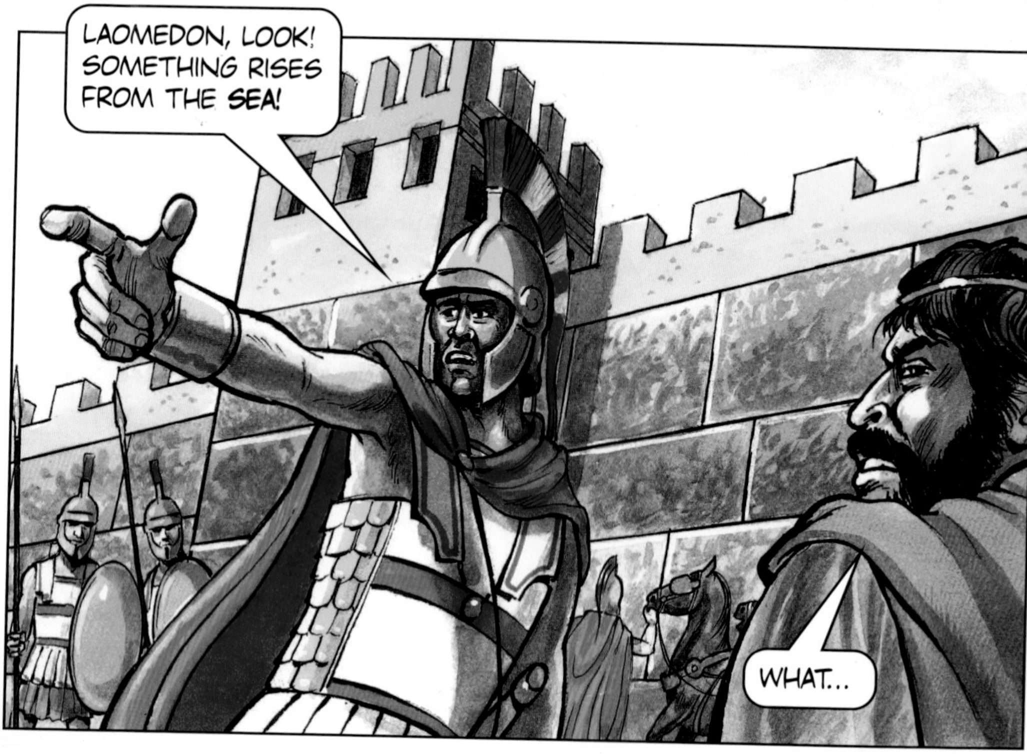
LAOMEDON, LOOK! SOMETHING RISES FROM THE SEA!
WHAT...

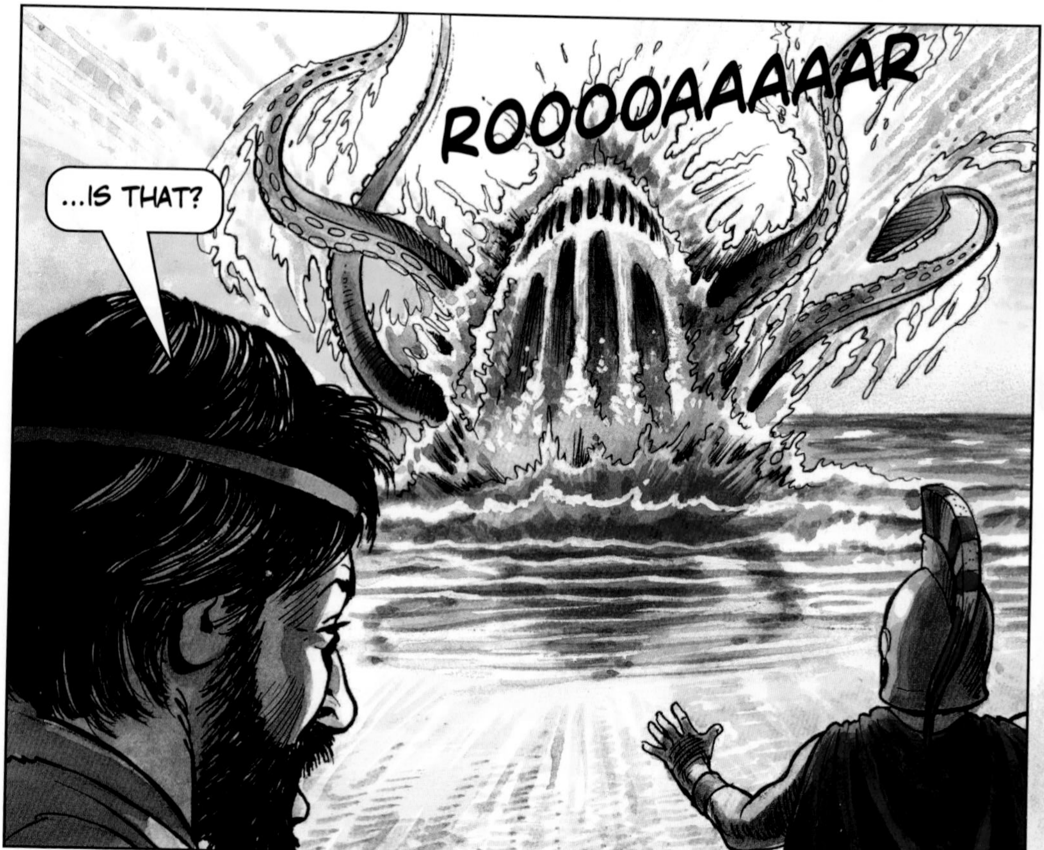
ROOOOAAAAAR
...IS THAT?

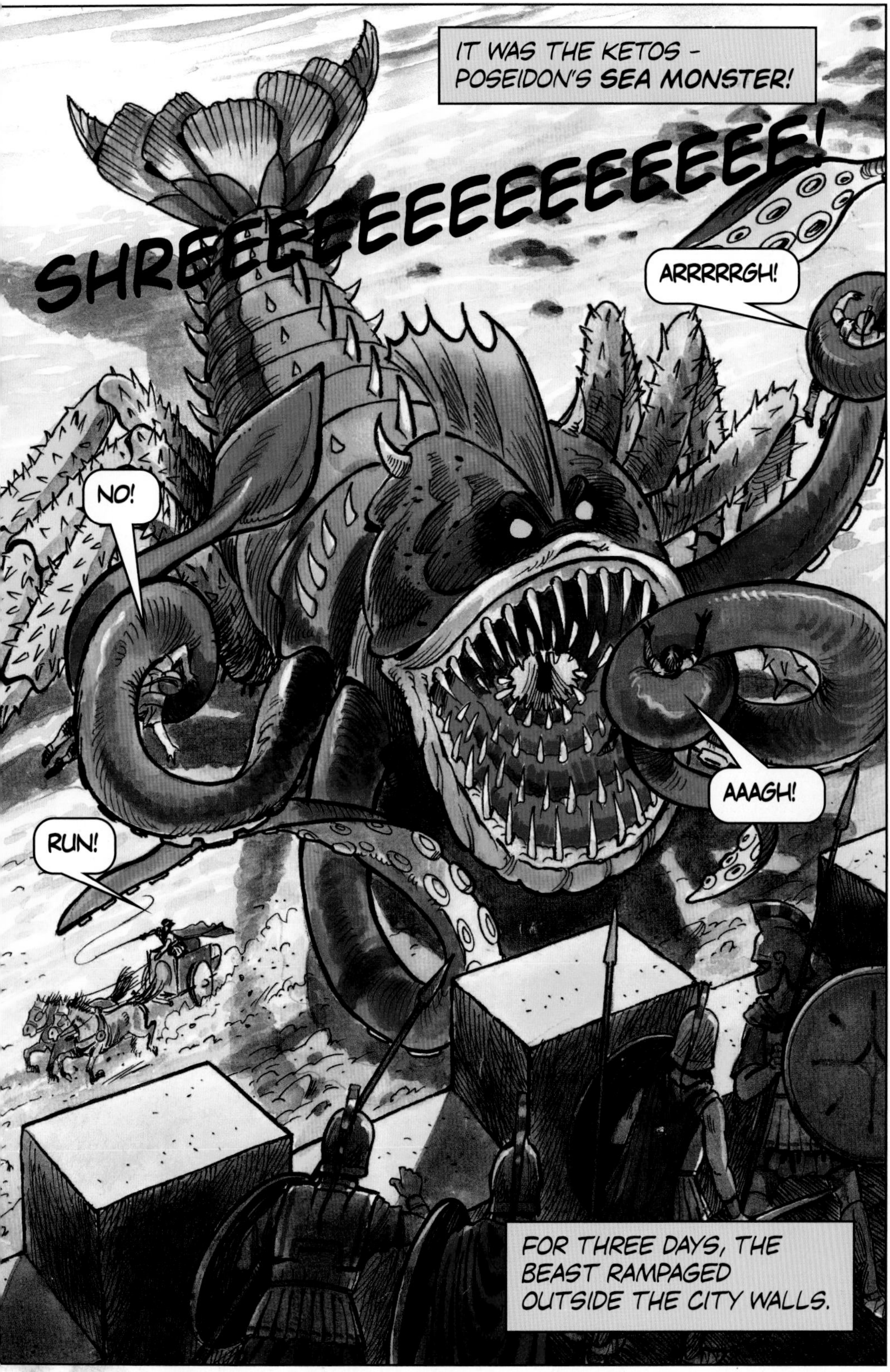
IT WAS THE KETOS - POSEIDON'S SEA MONSTER!
SHREEEEEEEEEEEEEEEEE!
ARRRRRGH!
NO!
AAAGH!
RUN!
FOR THREE DAYS, THE BEAST RAMPAGED OUTSIDE THE CITY WALLS.

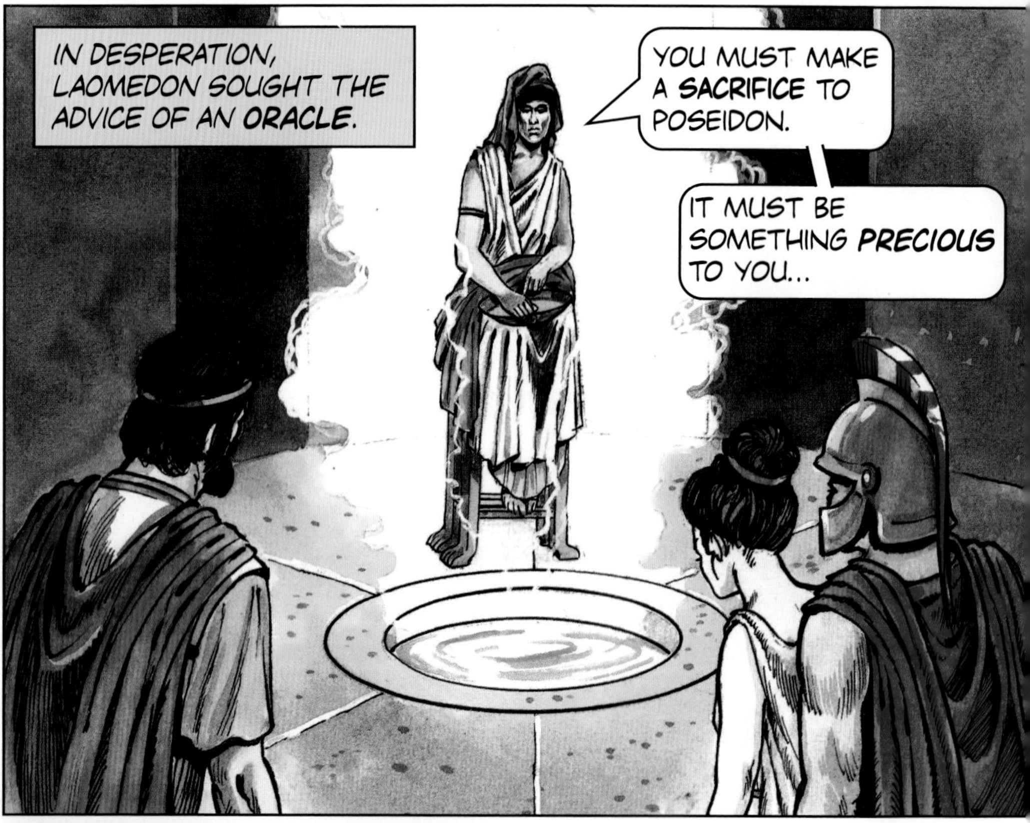
IN DESPERATION, LAOMEDON SOUGHT THE ADVICE OF AN ORACLE.
YOU MUST MAKE A SACRIFICE TO POSEIDON.
IT MUST BE SOMETHING PRECIOUS TO YOU...

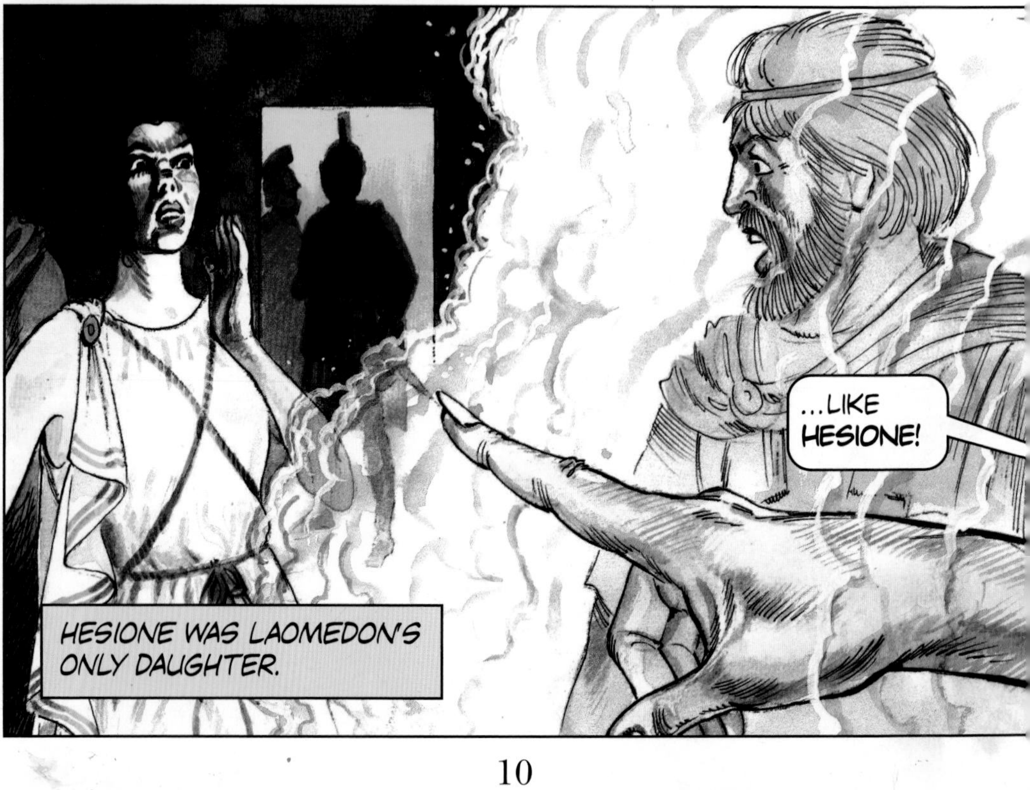
...LIKE HESIONE!
HESIONE WAS LAOMEDON'S ONLY DAUGHTER.

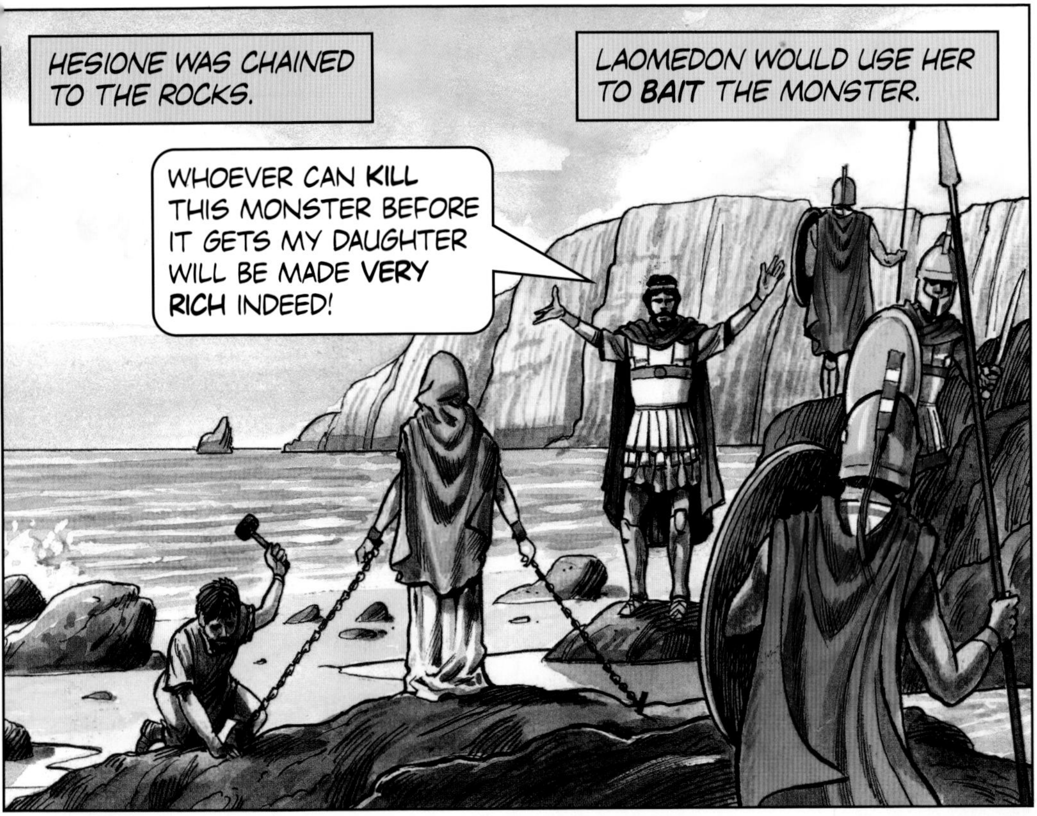
HESIONE WAS CHAINED TO THE ROCKS.
LAOMEDON WOULD USE HER TO BAIT THE MONSTER.
WHOEVER CAN KILL THIS MONSTER BEFORE IT GETS MY DAUGHTER WILL BE MADE VERY RICH INDEED!

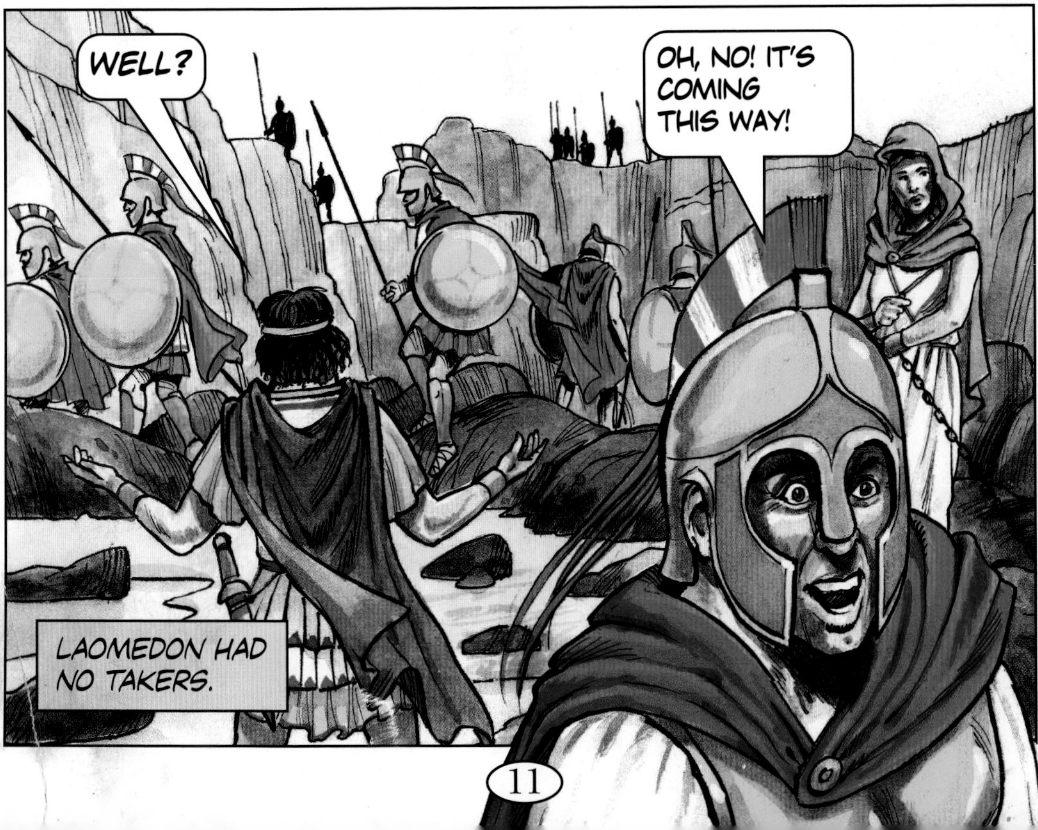
WELL?
OH, NO! IT'S COMING THIS WAY!
LAOMEDON HAD NO TAKERS.

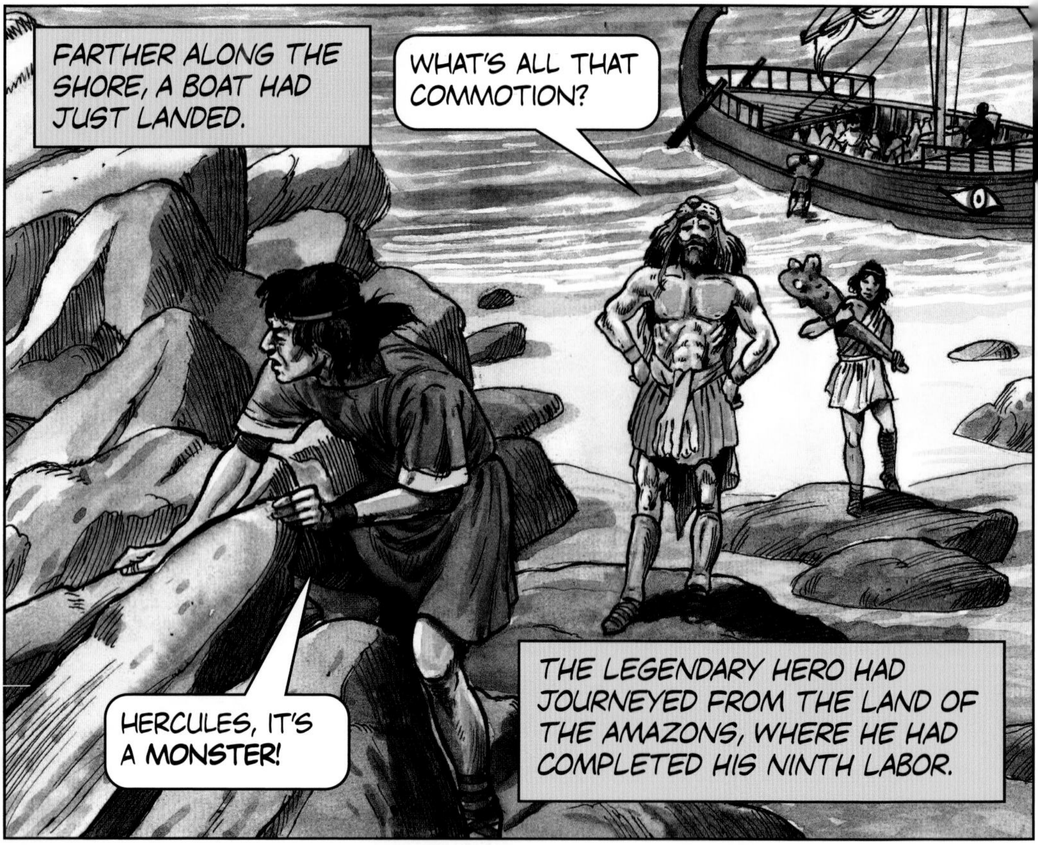
FARTHER ALONG THE SHORE, A BOAT HAD JUST LANDED.
WHAT'S ALL THAT COMMOTION?
HERCULES, IT'S A MONSTER!
THE LEGENDARY HERO HAD JOURNEYED FROM THE LAND OF THE AMAZONS, WHERE HE HAD COMPLETED HIS NINTH LABOR.

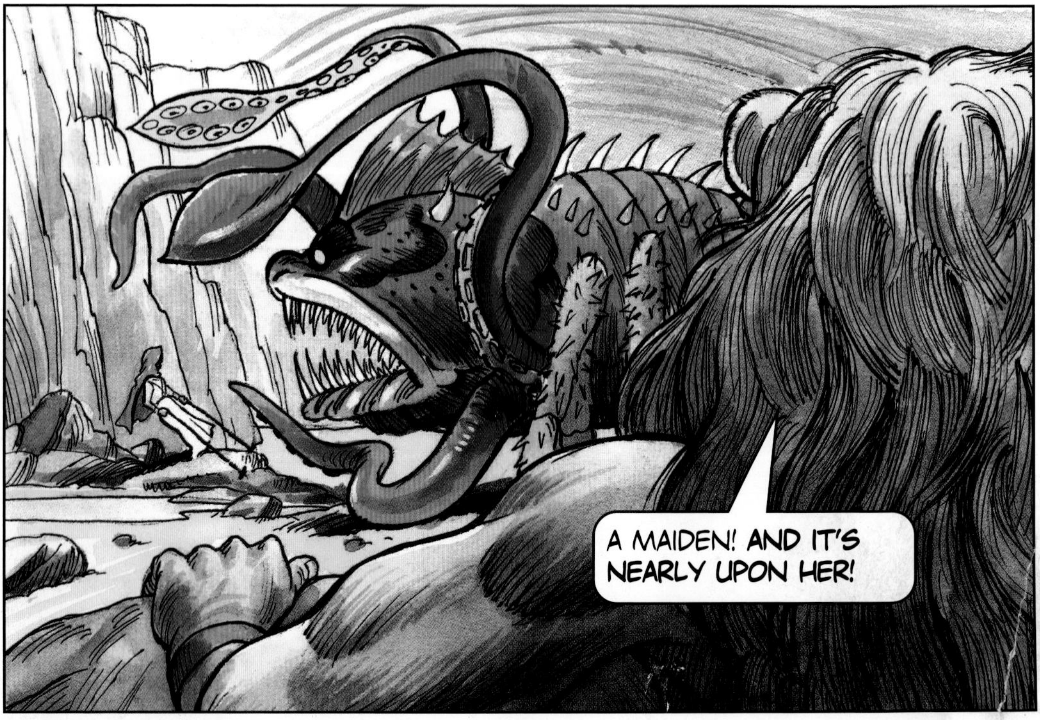
A MAIDEN! AND IT'S NEARLY UPON HER!

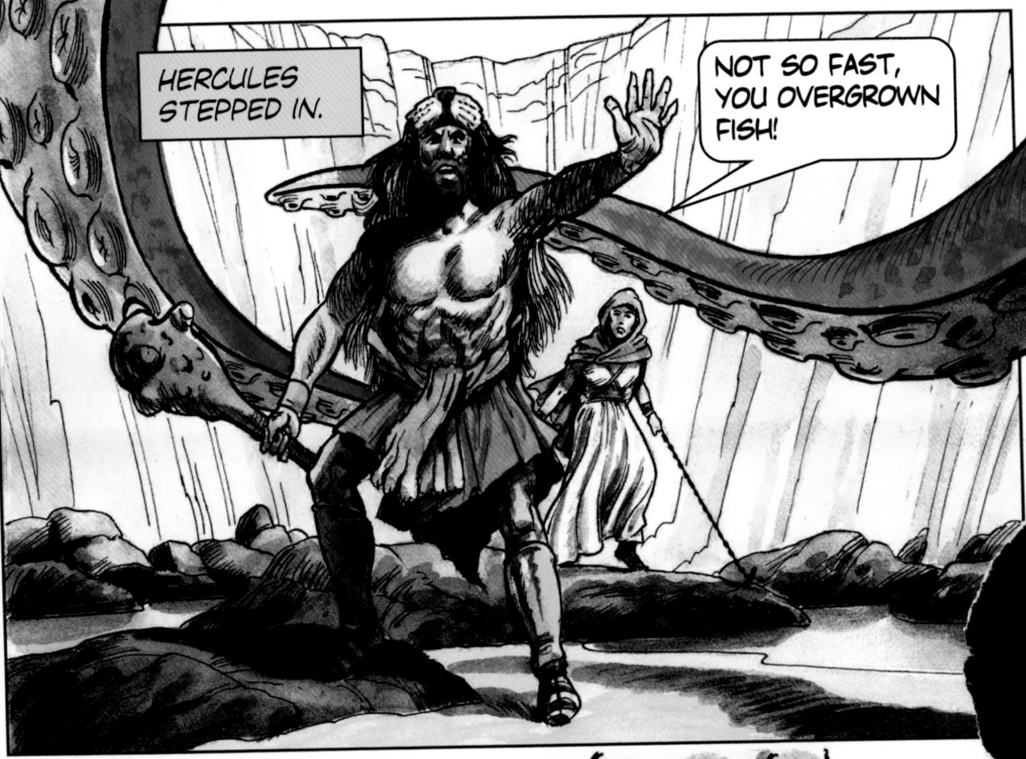
HERCULES STEPPED IN.
NOT SO FAST, YOU OVERGROWN FISH!

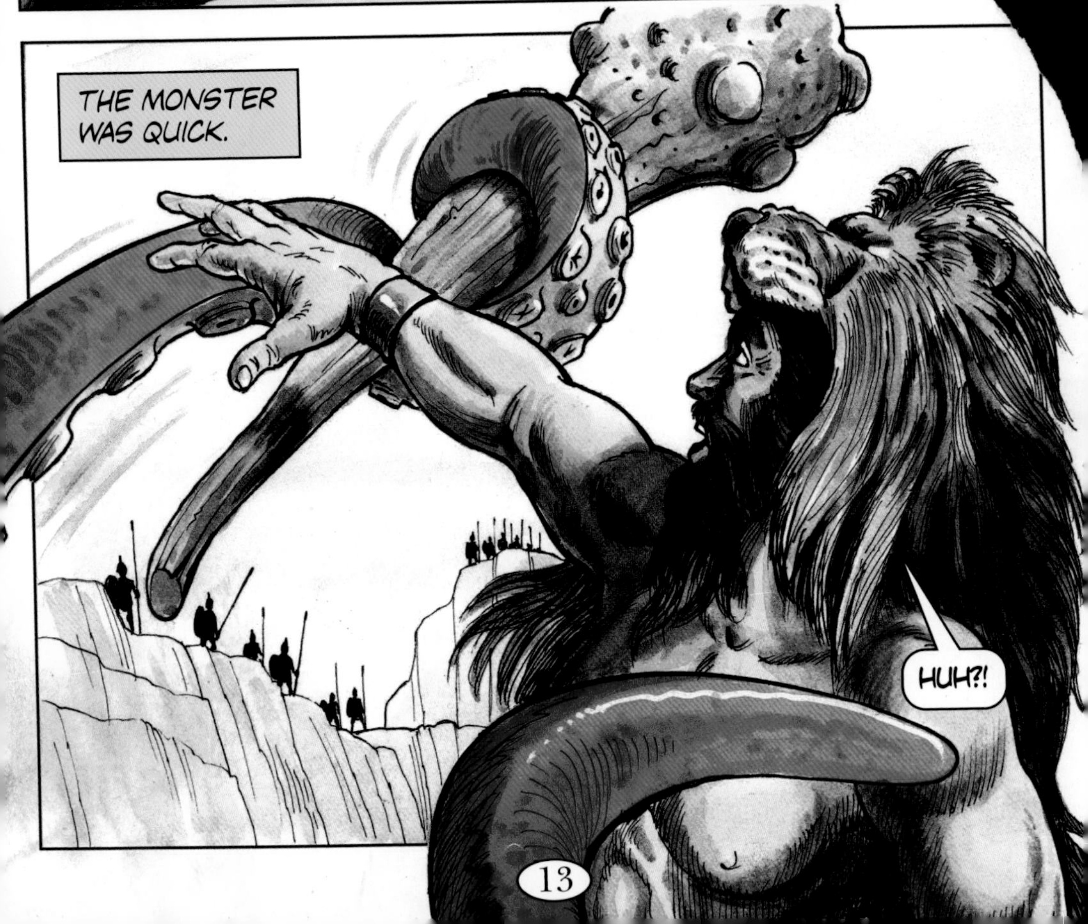
THE MONSTER WAS QUICK.
HUH?!

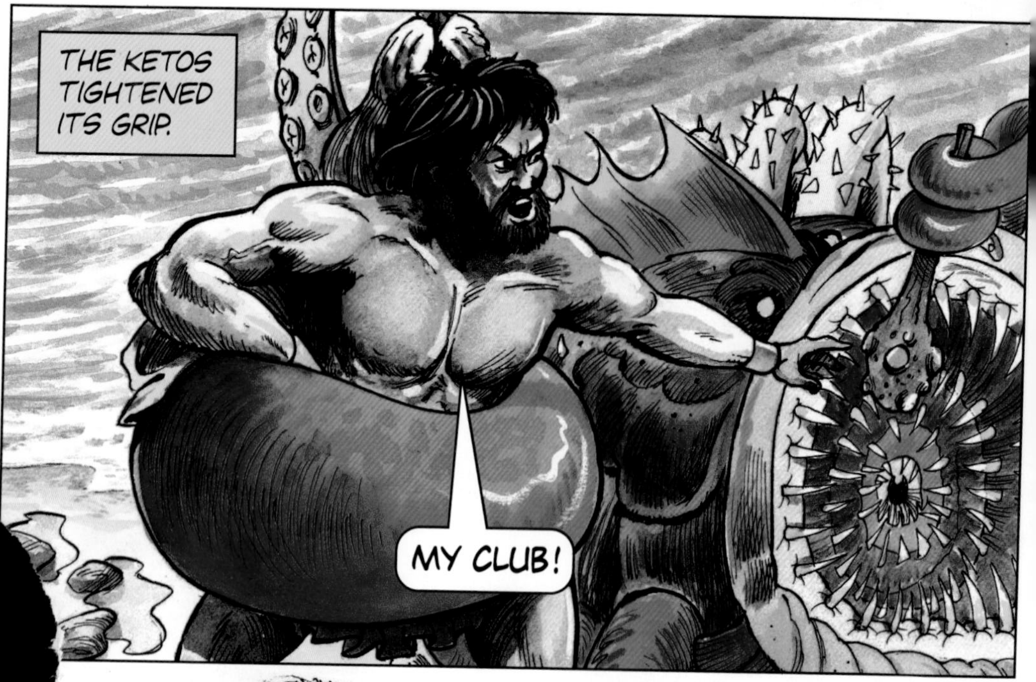
THE KETOS TIGHTENED ITS GRIP.
MY CLUB!

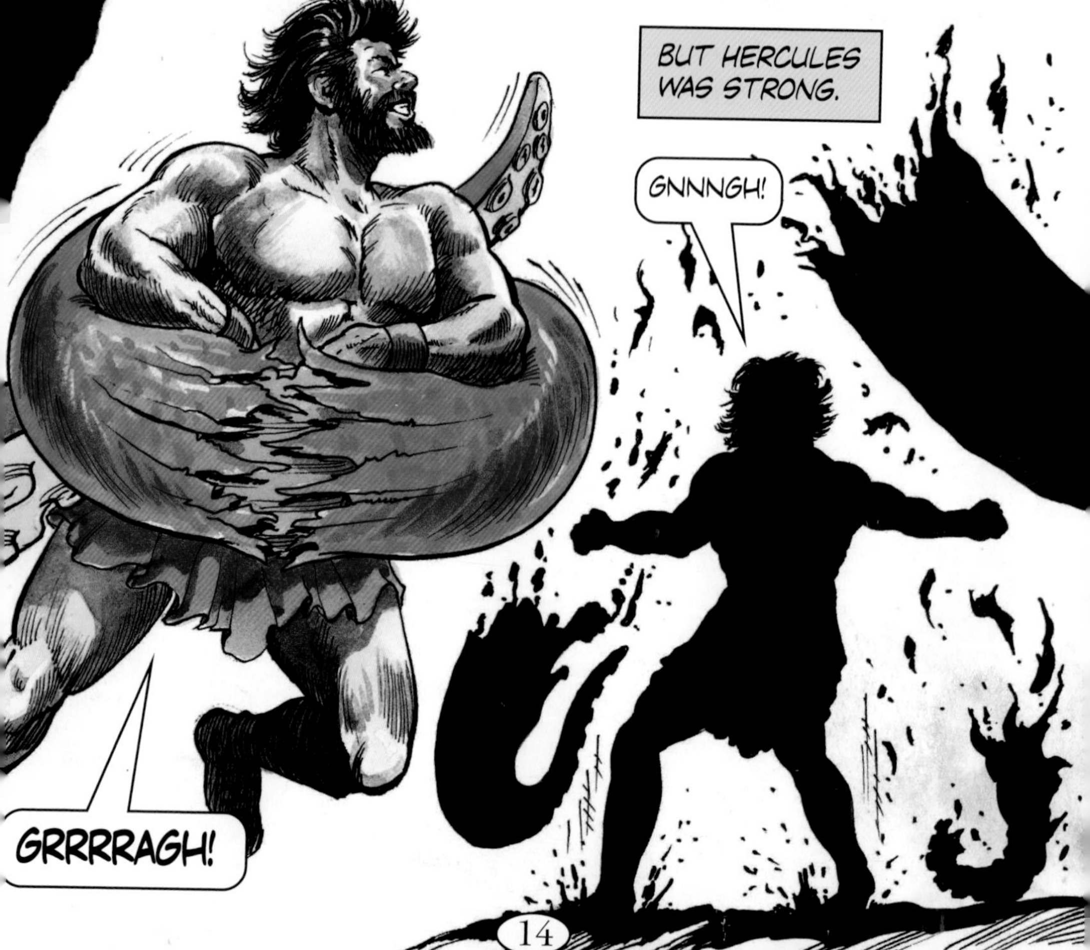
BUT HERCULES WAS STRONG.
GRRRRAGH!
GNNNGH!

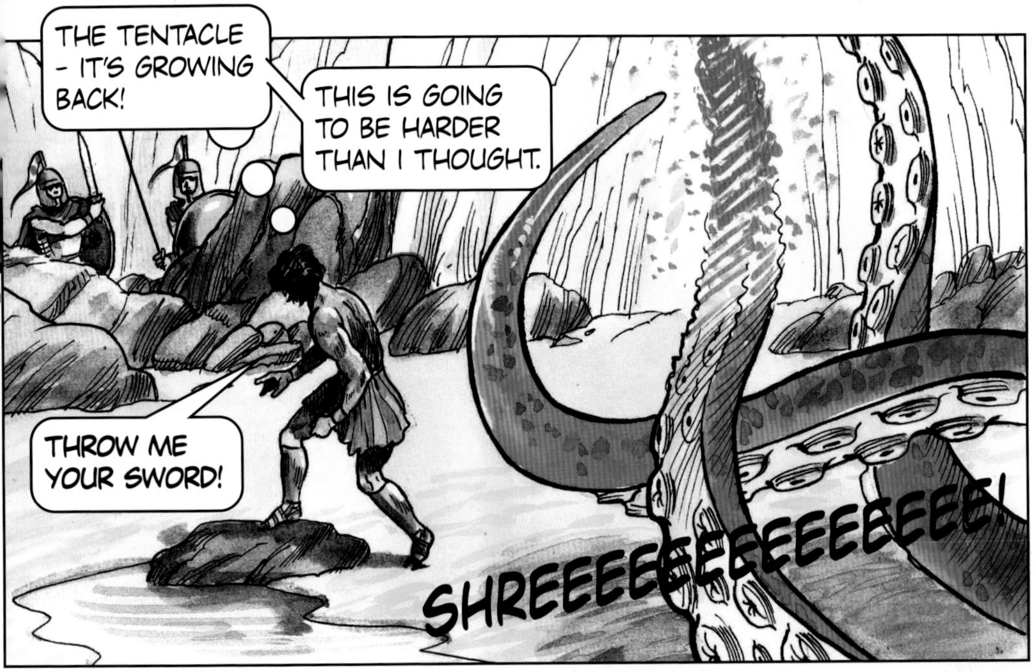
THE TENTACLE - IT'S GROWING BACK!
THIS IS GOING TO BE HARDER THAN I THOUGHT.
THROW ME YOUR SWORD!
SHREEEEEEEEEEEEEEEE!

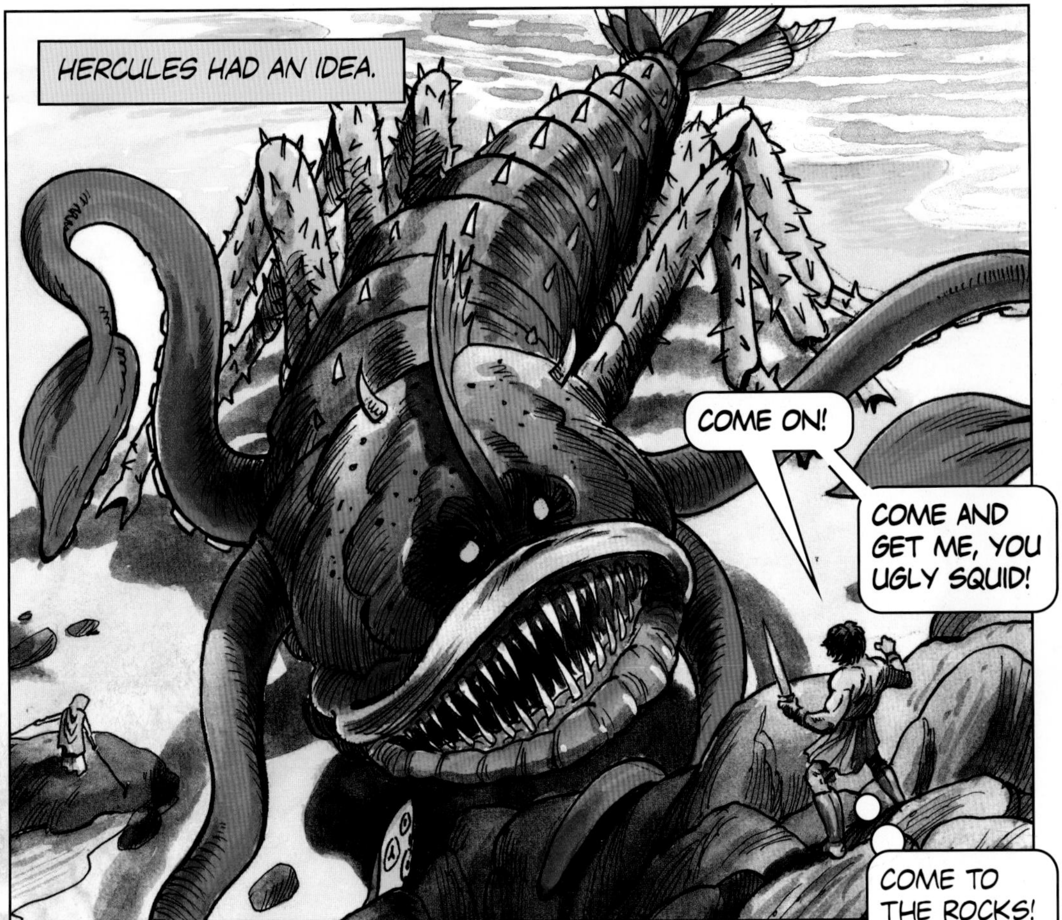
HERCULES HAD AN IDEA.
COME ON!
COME AND GET ME, YOU UGLY SQUID!
COME TO THE ROCKS!

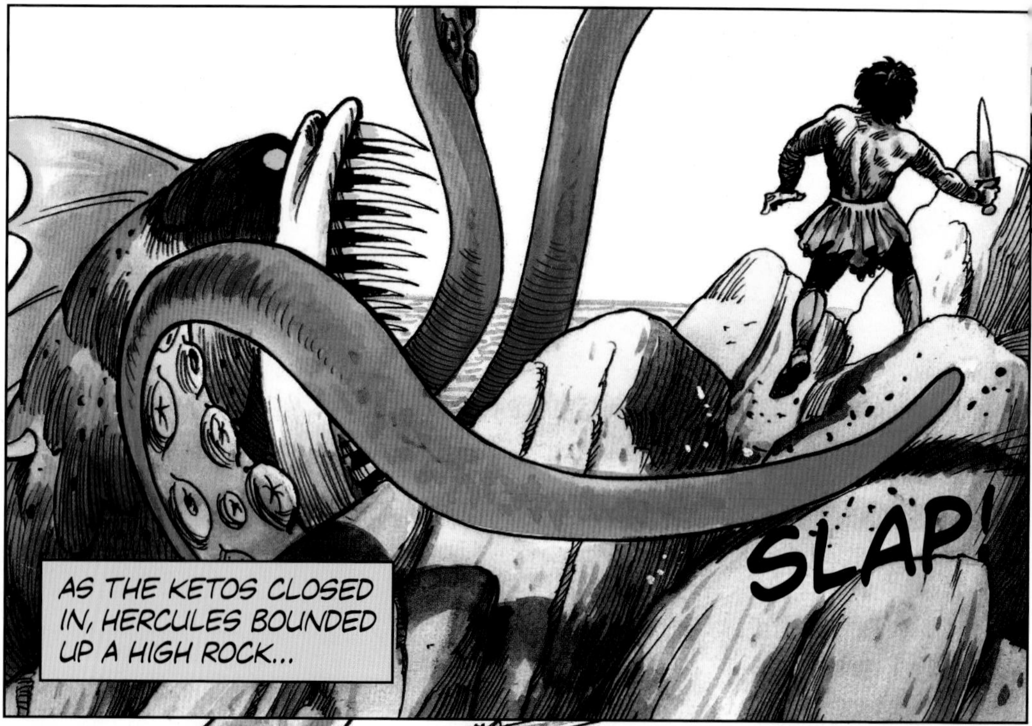
AS THE KETOS CLOSED IN, HERCULES BOUNDED UP A HIGH ROCK...
SLAP!

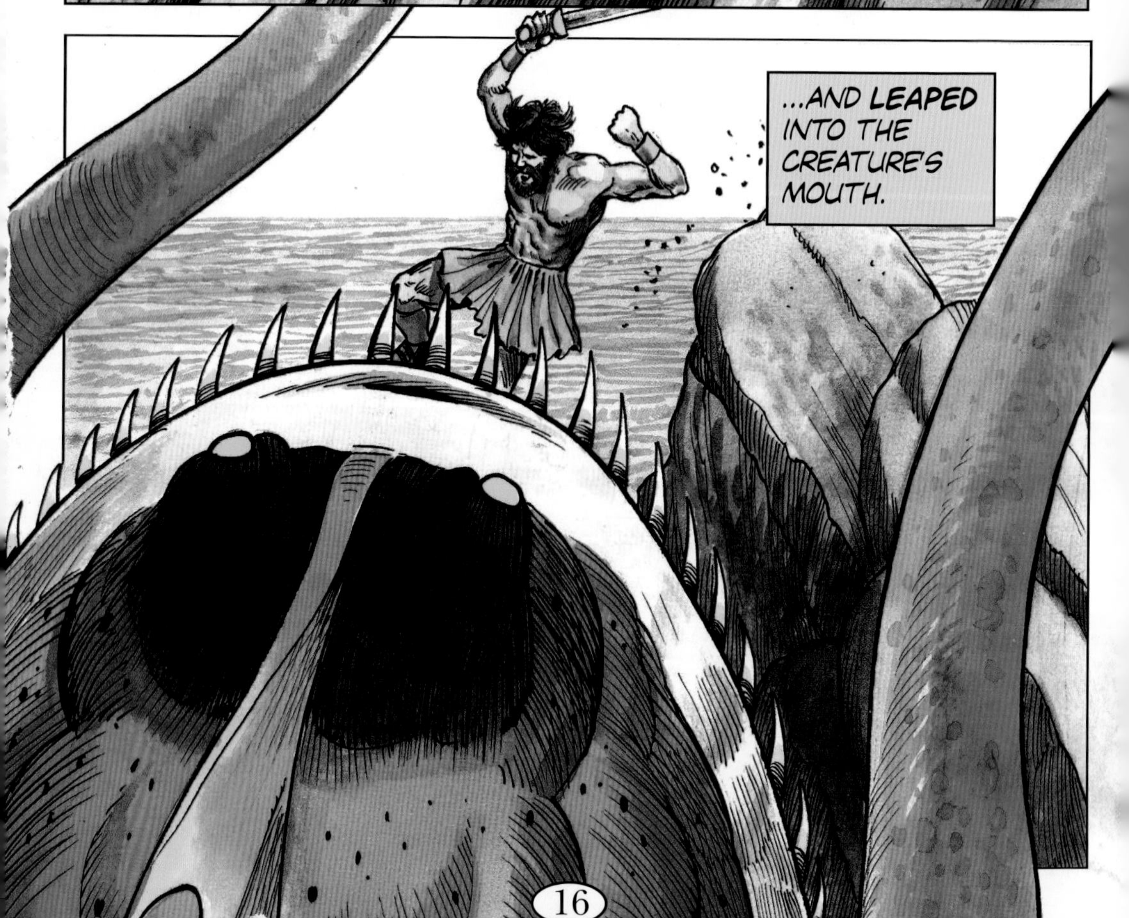
...AND LEAPED INTO THE CREATURE'S MOUTH.

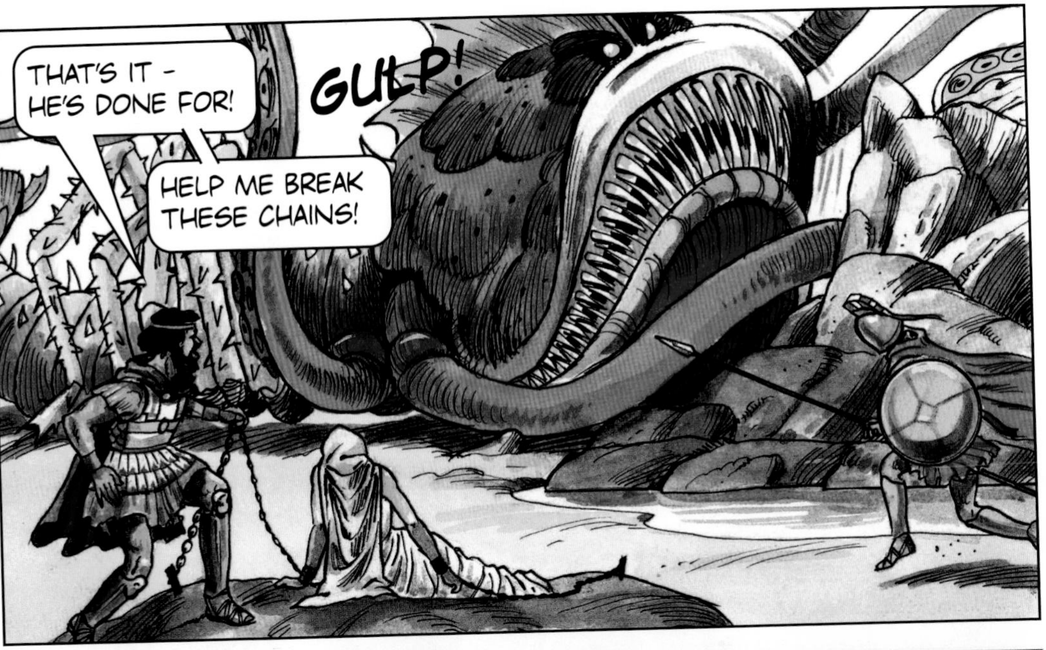
THAT'S IT - HE'S DONE FOR!
GULP!
HELP ME BREAK THESE CHAINS!

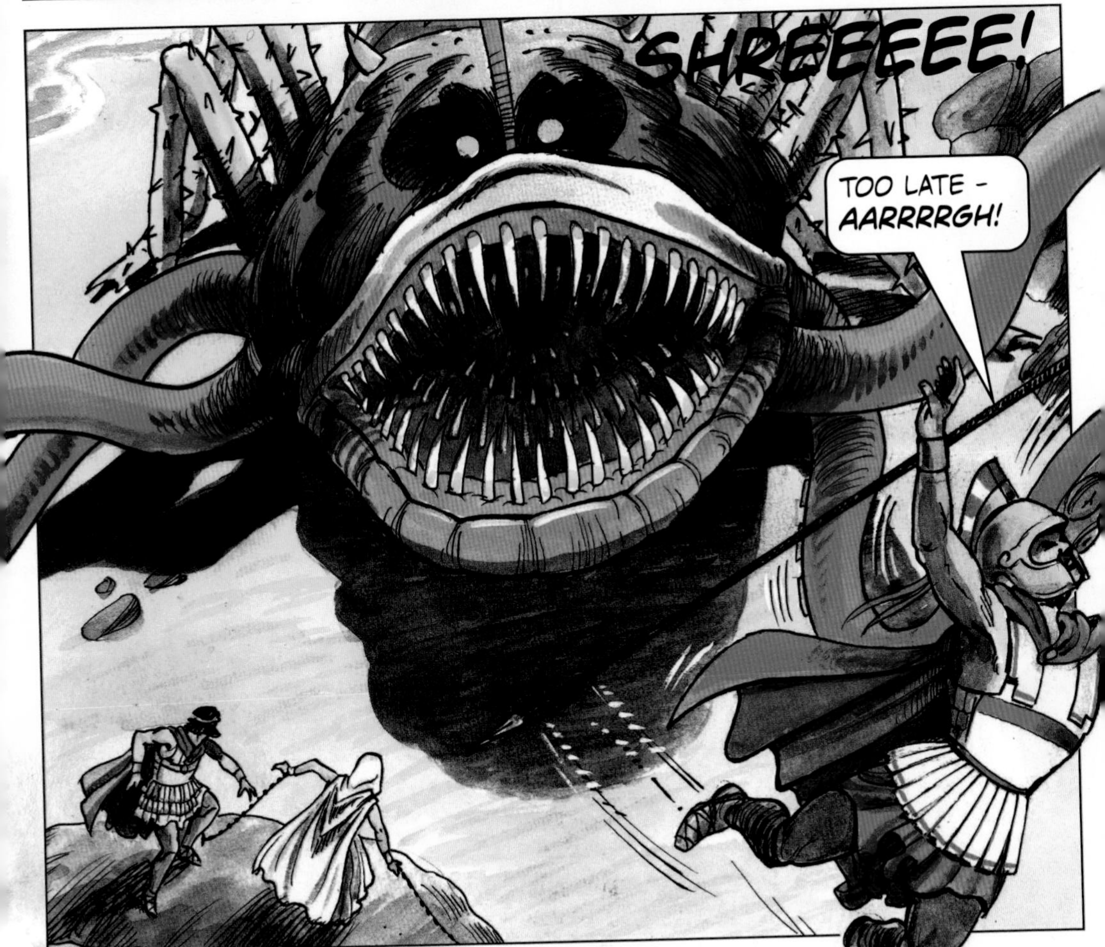
SHREEEEE!
TOO LATE - AARRRRGH!

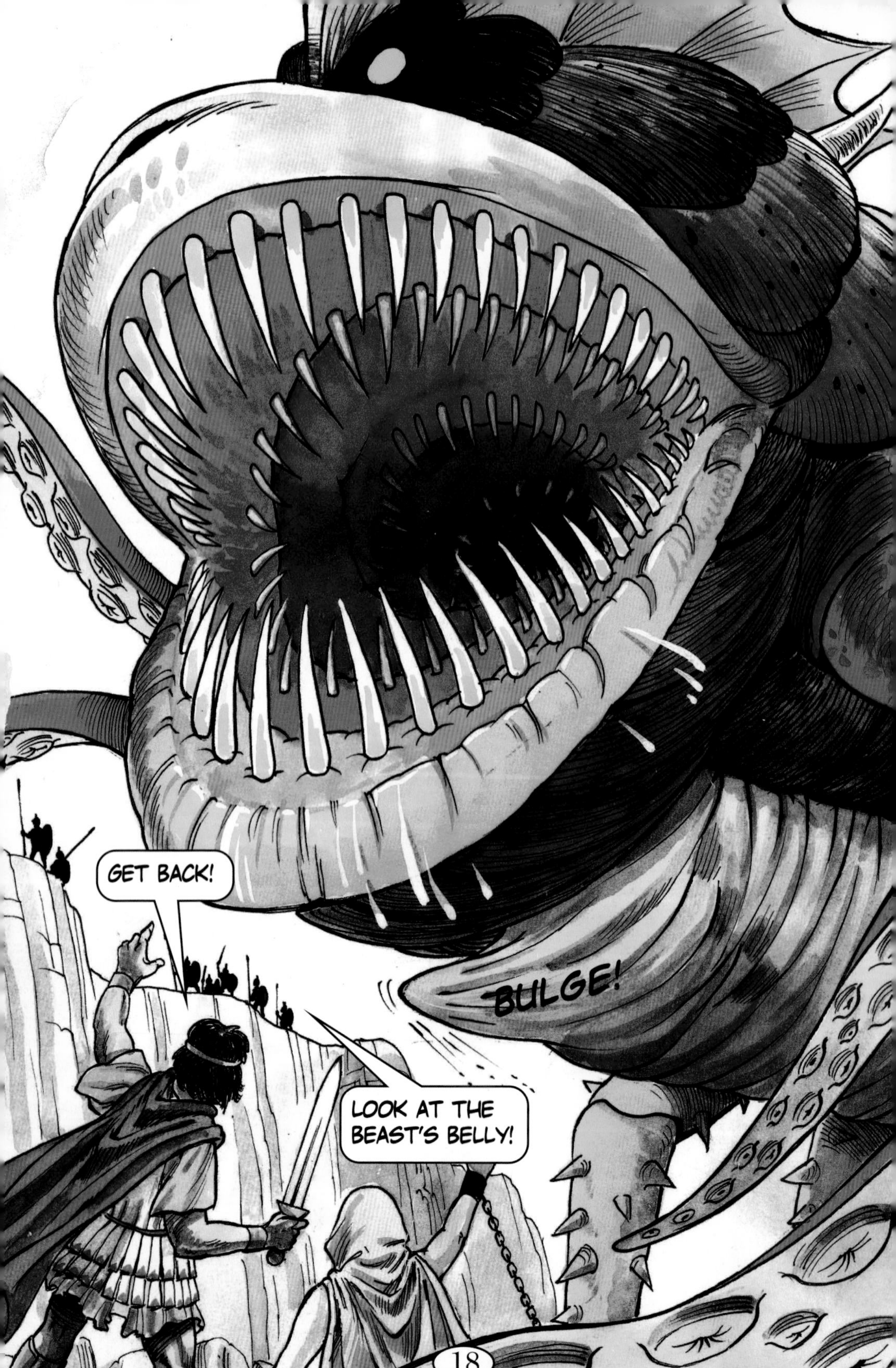
GET BACK!
BULGE!
LOOK AT THE BEAST'S BELLY!

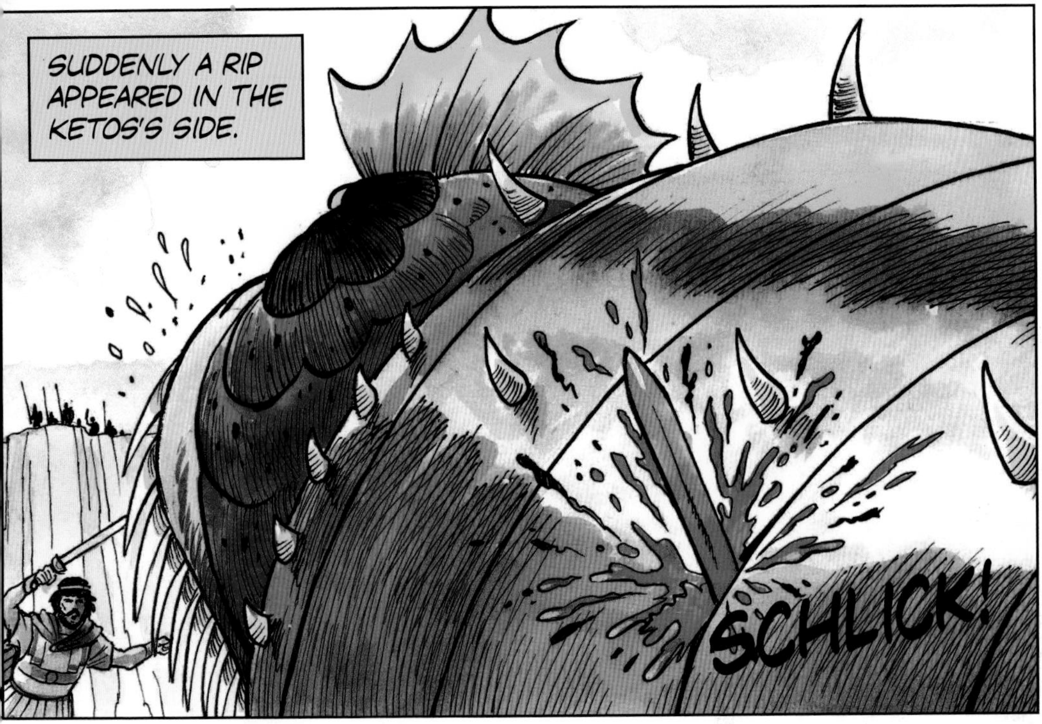
SUDDENLY A RIP APPEARED IN THE KETOS'S SIDE.
SCHLICK!

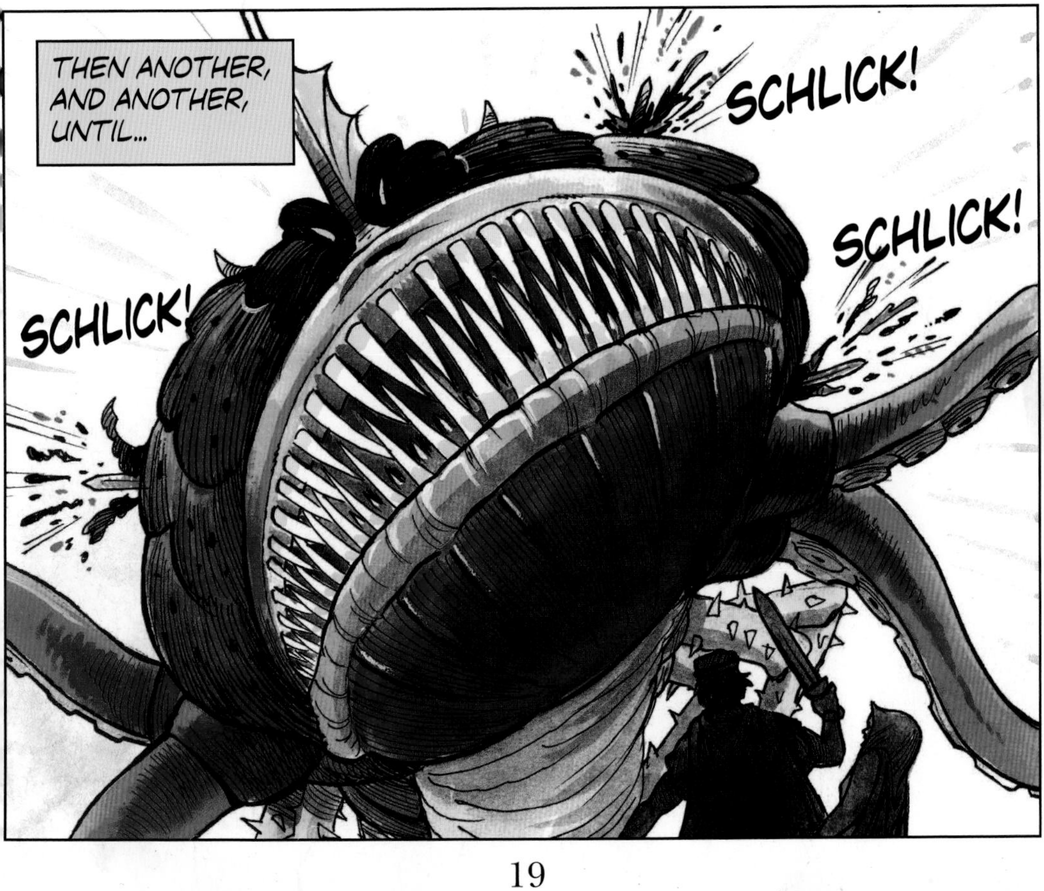
THEN ANOTHER, AND ANOTHER, UNTIL...
SCHLICK!
SCHLICK!
SCHLICK!

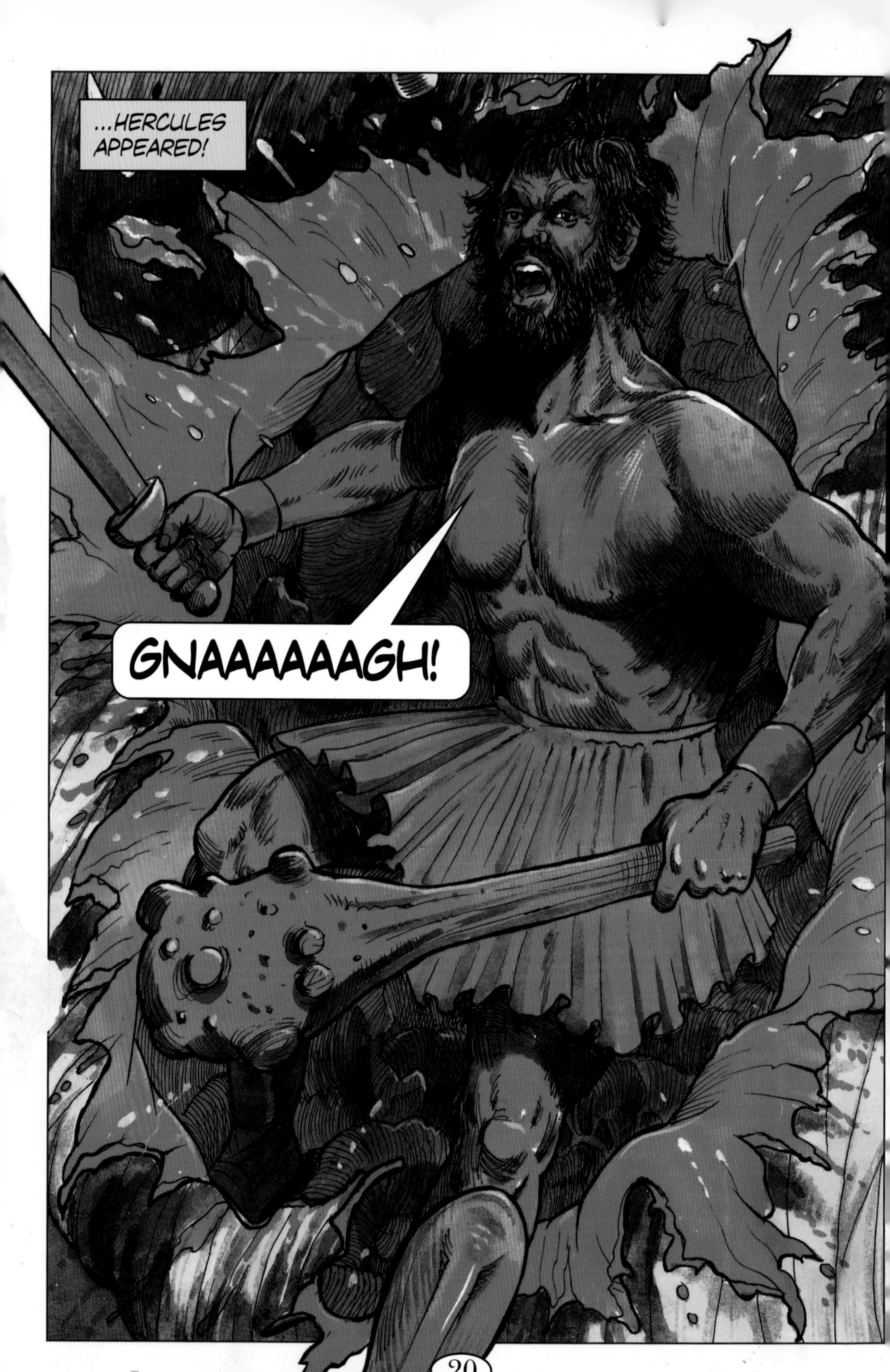
...HERCULES APPEARED!
GNAAAAAAAGH!

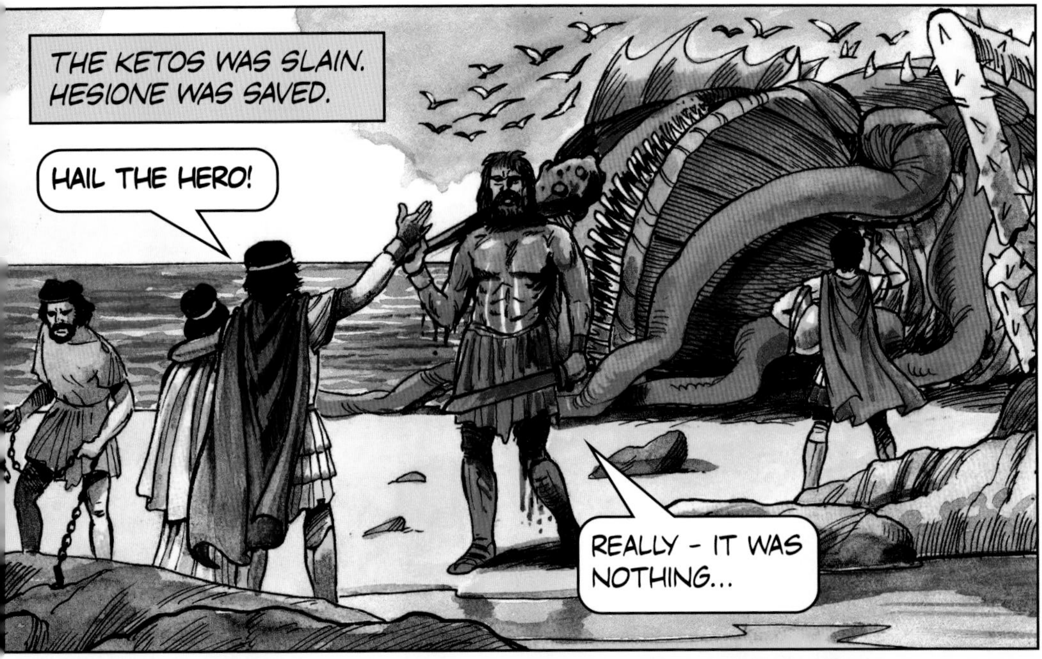
THE KETOS WAS SLAIN. HESIONE WAS SAVED.
HAIL THE HERO!
REALLY - IT WAS NOTHING...

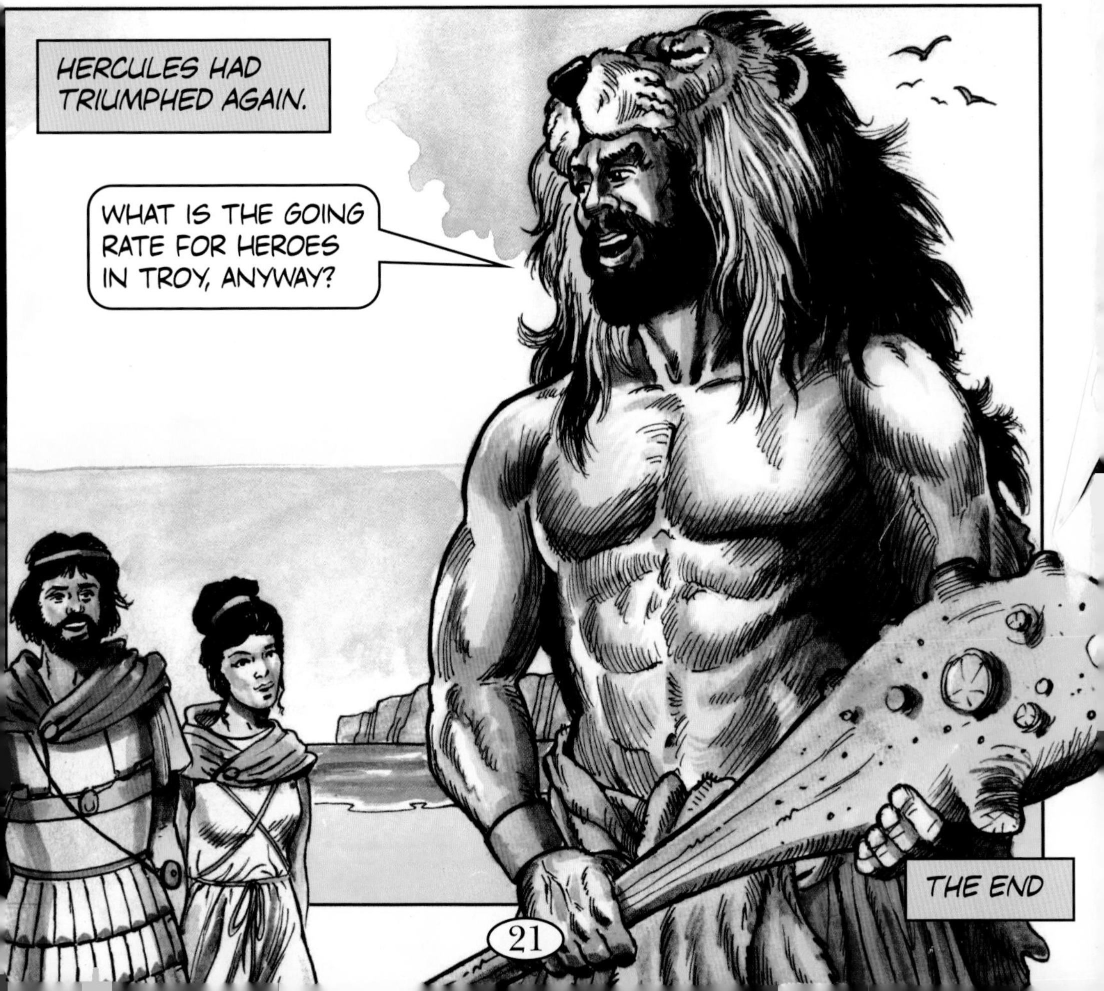
HERCULES HAD TRIUMPHED AGAIN.
WHAT IS THE GOING RATE FOR HEROES IN TROY, ANYWAY?
THE END

Hercules later fell out with King Laomedon over payment for his feat. However, it takes a big hero to beat a Leviathan or serpent, as you will find if you seek out these other legends.

Leviathan
In a battle at the beginning of time, the Hebrew God, Yahweh, conquers a huge sea monster that is bent on causing chaos.

Jonah and the Whale
The famous story of a prophet who is thrown overboard by superstitious sailors for causing a storm. In the sea, he is swallowed by a big fish, which saves him but also leaves him trapped.

Saint Columba and the Loch Ness Monster
The 6th-century encounter near Loch Ness of a terrible water monster and a cross-bearing saint.

Scylla and Charybdis
Odysseus's men must find a safe passage between a many-headed dragon and a deadly whirlpool in Homer's *Odyssey*.

Thor Fights Jörmungandr
The final battle, in which the Norse god of thunder sacrifices himself to stop the serpent of the underworld from destroying Earth.

Thor strikes hammer blows at Jörmungandr.

GLOSSARY

Amazons A nation of female warriors in classical mythology.

commotion A noisy rushing about and disturbance.

hoax An act intended to deceive or trick someone.

lair The resting place of a wild animal or a place for hiding.

legendary Very well known and presented in legends.

maiden A girl or young unmarried woman.

oracle A wise person through whom a god is believed to speak and who can see the future.

prehistoric Relating to the period before recorded history.

rampage To rush about violently or in a rage.

sacrifice The act of offering the life of a person or animal to honor a god.

seafarer A sailor or someone who travels by the sea.

superstitious Inclined to believe in charms, omens, and the supernatural.

tentacles Long, thin flexible limbs that grow from the head of some sea creatures.

INDEX

A
Amazons, 12
Apollo, 6

B
beast, 5, 9, 18

C
chains, 11, 17
Charybdis, 22

D
dragon, 22

H
Hebrew, 22
Hercules, 12–22
hero, 12, 21–22
Hesione, 10–11, 21
HMS *Daedalus*, 4
Homer's *Odyssey*,
    22

J
Jonah, 22
Jörmungandr, 22

K
Ketos, 9, 14, 16, 19,
    21
Kraken, 5

L
lake monsters, 5
Laomedon, 6–8,
    10–11, 22
Leviathan, 4, 22
Loch Ness, 5, 22

M
monster, 4–5, 9,
    11–13, 22

N
Norse, 22

O
ocean, 4
octopus, 5
Odysseus, 22
oracle, 10

P
Poseidon, 6–7, 9–10
prophet, 22

S
Saint Columba, 22
Scandinavia, 5
Scylla, 22
seafarers, 4
sea serpent, 4, 22
squid, 5, 15

T
tentacle, 15
Thor, 22
Troy, 6, 21

U
underworld, 22

W
whales, 4, 22
whirlpool, 5

Y
Yahweh, 22